FOLLOW THAT CAR

For Sarah.
Special thanks to Andreas Schuster,
Max Fiedler and Paul Breuer
S.L.

First published 2015 by Nosy Crow Ltd
The Crow's Nest, 10a Lant Street
London SE1 1QR
www.nosycrow.com

ISBN 978 0 85763 384 2 (HB)
ISBN 978 0 85763 385 9 (PB)

Nosy Crow and associated logos are trademarks
and/or registered trademarks of Nosy Crow Ltd

Printed in China
Papers used by Nosy Crow are made from wood grown in sustainable forests.

10 9 8 7 6 5 4 3 2 1 (HB)
10 9 8 7 6 5 4 3 2 1 (PB)

FOLLOW THAT CAR

LUCY FEATHER   **STEPHAN LOMP**

Hey, you . . . yes, you!

Mouse needs **your** help and he needs it **now!**

He needs to catch Gorilla and he needs to be super-quick!

Are you ready? Then let's go!

FOLLOW THAT CAR!

Look, there's Gorilla, over by the café.
Can you see him? How will Mouse catch him?
Can you work out which route he should follow?
He certainly can't drive through that
big sheet of glass, can he?
But you'd better be quick —
gorillas drive really fast!

Uh-oh! Watch out, Mouse, this building site is really busy.
Look at all those tall cranes! Isn't it an exciting place?
Where is Gorilla now? Can you see him?
And which way should Mouse go? Why don't you
follow the white arrows? Mouse will have to drive carefully,
won't he? There isn't even a proper road!

Good driving! That building site was **very** dangerous. Can you see Gorilla? He's so far away!

Oh dear, how is Mouse going to get through the car park?

He'll have to go down the ramp because that green car is in the way . . . but where will he go next?

Keep moving, everyone, this mouse is in a big hurry!

There's Gorilla!

Can you see him too?

He's over there, by the carrots.

Oh no!

One of the roads is blocked.

Mouse will have to hurry . . .

but which way is the right way?

Don't forget those arrows!

It's a good thing you're here

to help, isn't it?

Look! Things are very busy at the railway station! There are so many trains and there's a car stuck on the railway crossing, too! Where is Gorilla now? Can you see him? There he is, looking at his map. You'll have to show Mouse which way to go. Can you see a tunnel somewhere?

Well done
for spotting that tunnel
but Mouse still needs your help.
Gorilla's getting away! Can you see him?
Uh-oh, there's a tractor in the way,
and there are sheep everywhere, too.
If we're lucky, there might be a short cut.
Can you find one? Quick, let's catch that
Gorilla as soon as we can!

There's Gorilla!

Can you see him? He's nearly in
the mountains and Mouse has got a very
long way to go, hasn't he? He'll have to drive through
the market, but it's full of stalls and animals.
Can you help work out which way he should go?
Just watch out for all those barrels!

Phew! These mountain roads look hard work, don't they? But not for Gorilla — he's speeding away. Can you see him? But there's been an avalanche since Gorilla went past, and now Mouse can't go that way. Maybe there's another road Mouse can take. Can you find it? Be careful! The roads are very steep!

Brrr, it's pretty chilly here, isn't it? And look where Gorilla is now!

Can you see him? Oh dear, poor Mouse is still a long, long way behind him, isn't he?

Can you help him find a way through the ski resort? He certainly can't go straight on,

because there's a big truck in the way!

Wow! You're getting very good at this but look what's happened now! There's a traffic jam on the bridge and Gorilla has taken a short cut. Can you see him? Let's try and catch him up. Mouse will have to beep his horn to get past that red car, won't he? BEEP! BEEP! Watch out, Mouse, don't fall in the water!

Phew! Gorilla has stopped to get petrol. Can you see him? Quick, Mouse! You can definitely catch him up now! Can you show Mouse which is the right bridge to cross? We'd better hurry! **Hey,** Gorilla! **Stop** right there!

YOU FORGOT
YOUR BANANA!

Hooray! Gorilla has got his banana at last!

And it's all thanks to **you.**

You've been great at helping Mouse.

Come on then, everyone, it's time to go home.

But . . . oh no!!!!

Wait, Mouse! Wait!

You dropped your cheese sandwich!

Oh dear! You'll have to help Gorilla catch Mouse.

Are **you** ready? Then let's go!

FOLLOW THAT MOTORBIKE!